Short Bedtime Stories for Kids

Short Stories to Relax kid's and Toddler's Minds, a Collection for Children of all Ages!

Serena Hansen

Table of Contents

such, any inattention, use, or misuse of the information in question by the reader will render any resulting actions solely under their purview. There are no scenarios in which the publisher or the original author of this work can be in any fashion deemed liable for any hardship or damages that may befall them after undertaking information described herein.

Additionally, the information in the following pages is intended only for informational purposes and should thus be thought of as universal. As befitting its nature, it is presented without assurance regarding its prolonged validity or interim quality. Trademarks that are mentioned are done without written consent and can in no way be considered an endorsement from the trademark holder.

Introduction

Reading is the most important thing we can teach our children, reading is as essential today as breathing. Children will not be able to survive nowadays if they don't know how to read. We all know that learning and education begins at home. Parents should try to teach their kids how to read as soon as possible to provide them an edge when its time for them to go to school.

One way of encouraging kids to read is to read to them, the bedtime stories our parents use to read to us are not only to entertain us before we go to sleep but to also encourage us to learn how to read. Research shows that kids who read to by their parents when they were young are better at reading and studying.

Now as parents are duty is to provide reading materials to our kids that are tailored made for them. Reading materials that will encourage our kids not just to read, but learn about new things and acquire extra knowledge like about animals and their natural habitats. There are a lot of materials out there we can give our kids to encourage them to read. There are books, games, toys and many more that we can give them. But as we know, kids today have a very short attention span, if the thing we provide them does not interest them or intimidate them they will not even spend five minutes with it. Books are a good source of material that we can give to our kids, but most of the time kids find books intimidating and really boring because of the lack of visual materials. Kids learn better and faster if they have visual stimulation.

The art of telling a good bedtime story dates back quite far. This remarkable discovery speaks volumes as to the importance of telling bedtime stories to your child. Parents for literally thousands of years have told variations of the stories told today. It is an oral tradition of great importance and one that all parents should be doing. Not only is a bedtime story fun and relaxing, it is also an effective and important way to become closer with your child.

What Is a Bedtime Story?

Bedtime stories are stories that are told after your child has gotten into bed for the evening. Many times they will ask for you to sit with them. This is an easy opportunity to offer to tell them a story. Young children especially love this because it is a treat for them and makes them feel truly important at that moment.

You can either read a classic story from a book, find a quick one online, or tell one from memory. Oftentimes a great bedtime story is improvised to suit the mood of your child in that particular moment. These stories are typically ones that have been told for many years in many different ways. Popular stories include ones about princesses and princes, great monsters and knights, children on adventures, and exciting tales with no particular ending to them. This latter type of story is interesting because it allows you to draw the same story out over many nights to keep your child interested and always wanting more.

Develop Memories Together

Reading a bedtime story to your children is a great way to connect with them. It brings the family closer in an intimate setting that also makes the child feel special. Memories are made as stories are told. Your child will look forward to you sitting with them before they drift off to sleep. This time together is something that they will always cherish. These precious moments benefit everyone involved, and you will find that you look forward to the bedtime stories almost as much, or more than your little one.

Benefits Of Bedtime Stories

Telling bedtime stories is beneficial. Your child will find sleep coming in a peaceful way with a great story in their ears. It engages their imagination while giving them good dream material, and has been shown to calm down a busy child. Children do tend to be worked up at times, especially at night, and a nice story will put their fears to rest and allow them much-needed relaxation. You can make a story that shows them that the monster under their bed is not so bad, or that the shadows on their wall are their friends. The possibilities are endless with creative solutions to any nighttime issue.

Bedtime stories also teach your child in ways that are similar to fables, myths, and fairy tales. Reading bedtime stories is a compelling way of helping your child grow into a well-shaped individual. The fun part about bedtime stories is that you can make one up yourself and craft it into something unique and special. A special story goes a long way for a child with open ears, and you will become a source of great interest to your children.

The Winter Dragon

High on a cliff, overlooking the plain, the dragon Inferna had her nest - if nest was the right word for a few rocks balanced on a windy ledge. In it were four large, pointed eggs.

Over the years, the people of the scattered villages below had grown used to Inferna's presence. It was something they had learned to live with.

Once in a while, to be sure, some brave and foolish youth might vow to climb the cliffs in spring and destroy the eggs before they hatched.

And once in a while, his broken body might be found at the bottom of the cliff-face - or never found at all. So, on the whole, the nest was left alone.

This spring, the dragons hatched as usual: two males and two females. Inferna, their proud mother, watched the babies stumbling around on the rocky ledge. They were ungainly and quarrelsome, and already very strong.

As soon as they could speak, the baby dragons told her their names.

"Ferox," snarled the biggest, a handsome rust-red male.

"Atrox," croaked the other male, long and sinuous and orange as a flame.

"Dura," growled the third, a muscular green female.

"Nivalis," breathed the fourth, so softly that her mother could barely hear. She bent her head down to her daughter. "Nobilis?" she asked her hopefully. "Mirabilis?"

"Nivalis," whispered the baby dragon.

Inferna had never heard this name before. This did not surprise her; she had never seen a dragon like Nivalis either.

For her daughter was the colour of a cloud. She was not quite white, and not quite grey. Her eyes were of the same uncertain milky colour as her scales. When Inferna looked down at her own fiery red skin, and remembered the babies' handsome green father, Noxius, she could not understand it.

Still, what did it matter? All four dragons were healthy and growing fast. They were always hungry, so that very soon Inferna was hunting night and day to keep up with their appetites. Luckily the baby dragons were not fussy. They would eat anything that ran or hopped or flew.

Only Nivalis was proving awkward to feed. When the others tore enthusiastically at a lamb's carcass, she would pick at it half-heartedly. She preferred her meat cold-blooded: snakes, lizards and especially fish.

As the dragons grew bigger and the nest more crowded, the other three started to complain about Nivalis.

"She's always cold!" whined Atrox. "She makes me shiver!"

"Move over, then," Inferna snapped.

"Dura won't give me room!"

"I'm not going next to Nivalis," grunted Dura. "She chills me right through."

"Well, why should I?"

"I'm not," declared Ferox, "because I'm the biggest." Atrox bit him.

So it went on. Atrox tried to push Nivalis out of the nest when nobody was looking: but she gave him such a raking with her claws that he did not try again.

As they grew larger, the young dragons grew noisier as well. The evening air was filled with their harsh screeching as they tried out their voices. But the voice of Nivalis was as thin and clear as glass.

By early summer they were testing their wings, bounding up and down on the edge of the nest. It was none too soon for Inferna. She was exhausted by their ravenous demands. The sooner they could fly and hunt down their own food, the better.

Perching on the cliff-top, Inferna scrutinised the plain below. She saw tangled thickets hiding deer: coppices where the wild pigs scratched: and deep woods, where the wolves ran. Plenty of good food.

However, the forests could be dangerous - even for a dragon. They harboured giants and gryphons, witches and wodwos. So she preferred to hunt in the open fields around the villages, where men fattened their sheep.

Inferna's favourite village was called Great Toft. She regarded it as entirely her own territory, and fought off any dragons that came near. Next year, when her babes were fully grown, they would have to find new territories of their own.

However, five miles to the east lay another village, Little Toft. There had been no dragon there since old Belliger had died, years ago. Her little ones could practise hunting there, she decided. There were plenty of cows and sheep, and the villagers were as soft as butter.

It would keep her fledglings out of her way, and the strongest of them could eventually take the village over. She hoped it would be Ferox. He was her favorite.

Brand the Blacksmith of Little Toft was hard at work. He glistened with sweat as he bent over his anvil, hammering. His son Walter watched him, half-hypnotised by the heat and the steady clang of his father's hammer.

Straightening up, Brand dunked the red-hot iron into a bucket of water which sizzled and steamed.

"Take those spears to Weaver's house, while I get on with Merchant's. Much good they'll be - Merchant won't know what to do with a spear. Still, who am I to argue?" He wiped his face and neck on a cloth. "And George Farmer's got some daft idea about an iron fence. How is that going to keep a dragon out, I ask you?"

"At least these dragons are good for business," volunteered Walter timidly. He was somewhat scared of his father and of the raging heat of the forge.

"I'd rather have no business and no dragons. We've had no dragons at Little Toft these ten years, and we don't want them now."

"But we've often seen dragons flying around," said Walter rather wistfully.

"That's different. They weren't staying. We don't want dragons moving in."

Walter did not argue. He hefted the spears and went out of the forge into the cool, clean sunshine.

Weaver was not at home. He was probably at the market, but Walter decided against trying to find him in the heaving crowds of the market square. However, he could not just leave the spears, so he sat down by the front door to wait.

Closing his eyes, he let the sunlight shine red through his eyelids. In his imagination he saw the line of four dragons sweeping across the sky, just as he'd seen them last week: straight and swift as arrows shooting overhead. They had been wonderful.

The hubbub of the market turned to sudden cries of alarm. Walter opened his eyes, and beheld the dragons of his dreams.

His heart leapt as they streaked out of the clouds, blazing red, dazzling orange and iridescent emerald green. But the last one was a strange grey colour; he wondered if there was something wrong with it.

The dragons circled high over the market square and screamed. Down below the villagers screamed too, and yelled and shook their fists and anything they could lay their hands on: brooms and rakes and crutches. They threw stones and pots and potatoes up at the dragons - pointlessly, since these hurt nobody but the unfortunate people they came down on.

"Why all the fuss?" asked Walter. "They've hurt no-one except a couple of sheep."

"It starts with sheep," answered an old woman nearby, busy banging on a kettle with a wooden spoon. "They're only young."

Like me, thought Walter, as he dodged a flying potato. "But they're so magnificent," he said.

"You won't remember." She stopped banging for a moment. "You've never seen what a dragon can really do. To horses, cows - and people. We want to get rid of these dragons before they get any bigger."

By banging on a kettle? wondered Walter.

She pointed up triumphantly. "Look! They're leaving." The dragons were circling higher now. She shook her fist at them. "Go on, then, you vermin! And don't come back!"

The villagers cheered as the dragons soared upwards, shrinking.

The higher they rose, the lower Walter's spirits sank. He was bitterly disappointed to see the dragons go.

Then the biggest one - the red one - seemed to change its mind. Folding its wings, it dived out of the sky like an angry falcon, making the air sing. As it fell, it unfurled its talons, curved and cruel. It banked above the schoolhouse and raked its claws across the roof.

All the villagers ducked instinctively, apart from Walter. He was the only one to see the dragon draw in its breath and open its jaws wide to scream.

But instead of the expected scream, a long funnel of flame came out. It was hotter than his father's forge. It hit the door of Weaver's house, which smoked, turned black and went up in a roaring mass of flames.

Walter was the only one to see the expression on the dragon's face as it turned and wheeled back upwards. He thought it looked almost as surprised as he was.

Ferox had just discovered how to breathe fire.

"We'll never get rid of them now," said Walter's father gloomily, tossing pebbles into the duck-pond. "Not now that the orange one and the green one have learnt to breathe fire too. There'll be no stopping them."

"The fourth one can't fire-breathe yet," said Walter. "The grey one."

"What does that matter? Three are bad enough. Cornfields, haystacks, sheds, roofs, barns - nothing will be safe. Look at them," said Brand grimly.

Two dragons spiralled high: one emerald green, one grey, almost lost against the clouds. The green one swooped at a patch of woodland nearby, breathing a funnel of fire. The treetops burst into flame, causing half a dozen terrified deer to bound out from their cover.

The dragon dived and plucked a faltering deer from the ground. Then it took off across the fields, leaving a blackened trail across the wheat.

"It's nothing to them," said Brand. "Just wait until harvest. Every sheaf, every bale. We may as well not bother."

Now it was the grey dragon's turn. It plunged down - not at the trees, but straight at them. Walter heard the hiss of wind through its wings, before his father grabbed him and pulled him flat on the ground. There was a high-pitched shriek, a tremendous splash, and a great quacking of panicky ducks.

Cautiously he raised his head. The grey dragon was gliding away, a large fish squirming in its jaws.

"At least it can't set the duck-pond on fire," said Walter.

"I've seen a dragon fry fish in a pond before now," answered Brand.

Walter got up and walked to the water's edge. There were no ripples. The pond had an odd sheen. Then he saw the indignant ducks skidding across its surface.

"It's frozen!"

Brand poked it with a stick. Cracks spread across the pond, drawing a glittering maze.

"Well," said Brand, and did not seem to know what to say next.

"It breathed ice," said Walter. "Ice!" He picked up a piece of pond and held it, staring after the dragon, until his dripping fingers burned with cold.

However, one dragon that breathed ice did not compensate for three that breathed fire.

It was a novelty, certainly. The villagers now had ice at hand whenever the grey dragon went fishing: it was useful for keeping the butter cold and the milk fresh.

"But what good is that," said Brand, "when the others keep eating our cattle? We'll have no butter nor milk soon."

At harvest, Walter saw his father's worst fears confirmed. The dragons turned the hayricks into blazes that fired up spectacularly for a few hours and then kept smouldering for days. The air was permanently fogged with smoke, so that people went round with red-rimmed eyes, and coughing.

"But then we don't need the hay," observed Brand bitterly, "since we've lost the animals to feed it to."

House after house was abandoned as the roofs went up in flames; there was no straw to re-thatch them. Several families camped inside the school house, which was tiled. Miller's waterwheel, damp though it was, became warped by the dragons' heat. It groaned and stopped.

"What's the difference? There's little enough corn to grind in any case," Brand muttered.

Summer wilted into autumn. The villagers guarded their few remaining livestock like their children, bought expensive grain from neighbouring towns, and worried about the winter. But as the weather grew colder, the dragons visited the village less often.

"What's happened to them?" asked Walter, peering out of the forge. The sky was full of orange and scarlet, leaves flying on the wind: but no dragons. It had been a full week now since one had last appeared.

"They sleep through the winter, so it's said," Brand told him. "Nobody knows where."

"Oh... Then we'll be all right now," said Walter, trying to sound cheerful as he knew he ought.

But Brand did not sound cheerful. "They'll be back, come spring," he answered gloomily. "We can survive one winter. But how many more summers can we last?"

Deep in the rainy mountains to the west, a great cavern lay hidden underground. It was here that the dragons slept.

As the rain turned to sleet and the sleet to snow and hail, more of them gathered from far and wide. They lay in slumbering heaps, claws entangled, tails entwined, old enmities forgotten for the sake of winter warmth. The air inside the cavern steamed and smoked and reeked of sulphur.

Amongst all the sleepers, though, one dragon was restless. Nivalis shifted and rolled over, unable to sleep.

She was too warm. She'd been pushed to the edge of the cavern by dragons complaining of her chilliness; but even by the wall she was too warm. The smoky heat of her fellows was stifling her. It was hotter than the summer sun had been - and in the summer, she'd at least been able to cool herself by plunging into ponds and lakes.

The memory of that cool water made the cavern's heat too much for her to bear. Nivalis began to creep slowly and carefully away from the sleeping dragons. She felt her way along dark passages of stone, following the cold call of the winter air.

She emerged on a ledge high up on the mountainside. The sky was a heavy grey and snow was softly falling. Nivalis breathed in deeply. The icy air filled her lungs and rushed through her blood. She unfurled her wings and stretched them wide, letting the cold snow caress them.

Then she opened her mouth and cried in sheer pleasure at the cold: a long thin cry like the wind that echoed round and round the icy mountains.

No answering dragon cried back. Nivalis was alone. And she was suddenly very hungry.

Trudging home heavily from school, Walter glanced up to see a dragon burst from the clouds in a swirl of snow. It swept across the fields like a great grey blizzard, leaving behind it a trail of dead grass encrusted and brittle with frost.

Walter raised both his arms and yelled with delight; and the dragon wailed back.

The villagers of Little Toft, of course, were less than delighted. They did not know what to make of the dragon's return. At least this one posed no danger of fire, and little risk to the remaining livestock - for the dragon preferred fish from the duck-pond or the nearby lake.

All the same, a dragon was a dragon, and they were wary. Very soon their dark mutterings were justified. For it became clear where the danger of Nivalis lay: not in fire, but in ice.

She could do the work of a dozen hard winters rolled into a minute. Though she could not burn thatch, tiles shattered under her freezing breath.

She breathed down chimneys and put fires out. She froze the log-piles solid. Snow began to fall softly whenever she flew overhead. The villagers shivered by day and by night.

The baker could not keep his ovens hot, so there was no bread. Water froze in pails, and milk in churns.

And at the blacksmith's forge, the furnace was extinguished and could not be relit.

"We've got to do something!" said Walter.

"But what?" said Brand listlessly. The fire in him had gone out along with his furnace. He looked small and grey and weary. Walter had never seen him like this.

"Don't worry!" he told Brand. "I'll go and talk to this dragon."

"Talk to a dragon!" Brand was jolted out of his apathy. "You can't just go and have a little chat with a dragon!"

Walter didn't see why not. "Well, it can't burn me up," he said, "and I doubt if it'll eat me, since I'm not a fish."

"It could freeze you to death!"

"I'll wrap up well."

Brand struggled to his feet. "I forbid it," he said hoarsely. "You're my only son, and you are not to talk to dragons. Do you hear me, Walter?"

"I hear you," Walter said.

Walter wrapped up well. Since his father thought he was going to school, he had to smuggle the extra clothes out of the house in a bulging school-bag. Once he was well away from the house, he headed to the lake.

Here, he stopped to put on two more pairs of trousers, two pairs of socks, an extra tunic, a woolly waistcoat and two overcloaks. By then he was so bundled up, he could hardly move.

He wrapped a scarf around his head and waddled down to the lakeside. The marshy ground was as hard as stone, with clumps of reed poking sadly through the frozen mud.

A few snowflakes were blown around in the bitter wind. Even inside all his layers, Walter began to shiver. He stamped his feet and squinted at the sky, wondering how long he would have to wait.

Not long. Out of the clouds it fell without warning. It must have been up there all along, perfectly camouflaged.

Wings folded, it dived straight at the lake. It crashed deafeningly through the splintering ice and disappeared underwater. Walter gaped at the swirling waves for a long minute until the surface exploded and the dragon re-emerged with a large pike thrashing in its jaws. As the waves settled, long fingers of ice were already groping across the water's surface to lock it up again.

The dragon landed on the shore close by and shook itself. Walter was sprayed with hail. As the dragon began to tear at the fish, he approached it cautiously.

"Dragon?"

It glanced up. "Human," it said without interest, in a thin, distant voice.

"I'm Walter. I'd like to talk to you."

The dragon gulped down the head of the pike. "So talk," it said.

"It's about my village."

"My village," corrected the dragon.

"But it's no use to you! You only eat fish. Why can't you leave us alone?"

"You're my village, for now at least," repeated the dragon in its chilly voice. "A dragon has to have a village. My mother told me. You're my territory. Do you think I like the place? Ovens everywhere, and horrible warm smoke coming up the chimneys."

"Is that why you keep putting all our fires out?"

"Of course it is!" the dragon said. "I hope I'm causing plenty of terror and hardship? Because that's what I'm supposed to do."

Walter opened his mouth and closed it again.

"Well, actually," he said slowly, "actually, we're quite enjoying it."

The dragon dropped its fish and fixed him with an incredulous glare from its icy grey eyes.

"Enjoying it?"

"Well, we like skating," said Walter. "And we like, er, making snowmen. And we can have ice-cream every day. And the butcher's ice-house is already full for the summer." This last fact was true, at least. "Oh, yes, we like the cold."

"You like it!" hissed the dragon. A blast of freezing air nearly bowled Walter over. He blinked as ice-crystals formed on his lashes.

"It's wonderful!" He tried to sound convincing. Although his mouth was so numb he could barely speak, he went on: "It's such a change from the usual sort of dragon."

The dragon drooped its head.

"And I thought you were all wretched and terrified," it sighed. "I'm no good at this. What use is it having a village if I can't terrorise it?"

Walter stayed diplomatically silent.

The dragon sniffed. "If nobody's afraid of me, I may as well go," it said tragically.

Even though this was what he'd aimed for, Walter felt sorry for it.

"Where will you go to?"

"I shall have to find another village." It sniffed again. "And you'll get another dragon."

"Will we?"

"Oh, yes. A village has to have a dragon, just like a dragon has to have a village. One of us will take you over. My mother said."

"What?"

"I know she wanted my brother Ferox to have you. The strongest and most fearsome, she told us. I rather hoped it would be me." Its wings wilted. "Ah, well. Maybe it will be Ferox after all. Though Atrox is definitely more fearsome."

"Atrox? Which one is that?"

"The orange one. He's got a temper. Still, that's not my problem." The dragon began to flap its wings, preparing to take off.

"Stop! Wait!" cried Walter. "Just a minute! If you won the village, would Atrox stay away?"

"They all would," it whispered. "They'd all have to find somewhere else."

Walter chewed his lip. "But how do you prove that you're the most fearsome dragon? I mean, apart from eating everybody up?"

"Erch! Eat humans?" spat the dragon. "No, thank you. Though I'm sure Atrox would gobble you up if he got the chance."

"Then he mustn't get the chance!" said Walter urgently. "How else? How do you decide?"

The dragon pondered long and hard. "Poems," it said at last.

"Poems?"

"So my mother told us. The most dreadful dragons have long poems written about them. Epics to enthral kings, and appal children on dark nights. That is how the fame of dragons spreads."

"I see," said Walter. "Yes. Thank you. Don't go away, will you? I'll be back."

Walter went back home and told his father, and Brand, once he had closed his astonished mouth, called a meeting of the villagers in the schoolhouse. There it was decided that a winter dragon was far preferable to a summer one, and that they should try to keep Nivalis.

Then all those who could read and write (mainly school-children) put their heads together to compose the dragon's poem.

It began like this.

Hark! For I shall tell you now

Of fearful monsters and of how

There came to us a more dread beast

Than any yet that from the east

Or north or west or south has come

To make this wretched place its home and nine hundred and twenty lines later, it finished like this:

And so this dragon holds us all

In its accursed and frozen thrall.

Proclaim its terror everywhere!

Beware! Beware! Beware! Beware!

Even though it had been written in a hurry, the school-children were very proud of it. It harped on a great deal about the ferocity of the dragon and the misery of the villagers. When Walter read it aloud to the grey dragon the next day, it took him the best part of an hour.

Nivalis was delighted. "You make me sound quite horrible!"

"Good. We're going to send copies to all the other villages," Walter told it. "Do you think that will do the trick?"

"If it doesn't, I don't know what will. It says such flattering things about me!" The dragon twirled her tail. "Do I really give all the children nightmares?"

"Dreadful ones," Walter assured her, and went so far as to clap her on the shoulder. This was a mistake: his hand froze onto the dragon's scales, and bled when he eventually managed to pull it away.

Spring came, despite the dragon, and the lake gradually thawed out with a great cracking of ice. Ferox, Atrox and

Dura awoke and came flying out of the mountains, trailing smoke, each intent on laying claim to Little Toft.

When they learnt of the epic poem, they were furious. They spat sparks and fizzed fire: but the poem was now famous throughout the land, and Nivalis was notorious as the Scourge of Little Toft.

"I don't care," grunted Dura. "It's only a common little village anyway. I can do better than that. I fancy a castle."

"I'm going to look for a proper town," said Ferox. "Somewhere with a few knights, a bit of excitement."

Atrox hissed in anger and thrashed his tail; but there was nothing he could do about it. So when the others departed, he had to follow them.

Inferna was very proud of her daughter, though puzzled as to just how she had gained such a fearsome reputation.

For with the coming of spring, the power of Nivalis waned. She could not compete with the sun. The frozen ground thawed out, the trees broke into leaf, and Brand the blacksmith lit his forge again.

By May, Nivalis had had enough. She was too hot, and she was tired.

So she flew to the high mountains in the west, and crept into the cavern, which was now silent, cold and empty. She lay down in the dark with a deep sigh of contentment, and closed her eyes.

In Little Toft, life returned to normal. The villagers re-thatched their roofs, counted their sheep and stored bushels of grain. There was much singing and merriment at harvest-time that year.

But Walter watched the leaves, waiting for the first rusty tinges to appear: waiting for the wind to change to its northern, wolfish howl: waiting for a grey cloud full of snow to sweep across the chilly sky and turn into a dragon.

The Fiery Dragon

The little Princess always woke in her little white bed when the starlings began to chatter in the pearl gray morning. As soon as the woods were awake, she used to run up the twisting turret-stairs with her little bare feet, and stand on the top of the tower in her white bed-gown, and kiss her hands to the sun and to the woods and to the sleeping town, and say: "Good morning, pretty world!"

Then she would run down the cold stone steps and dress herself in her short skirt and her cap and apron, and begin the day's work. She swept the rooms and made the breakfast, she washed the dishes and she scoured the pans, and all this she did because she was a real Princess. For of all who should have served her, only one remained faithful–her old nurse, who had lived with her in the tower all the Princess's life. And, now the nurse was old and feeble, the Princess would not let her work any more, but did all the housework herself, while Nurse sat still and did the sewing, because this was a real Princess with skin like milk and hair like flax and a heart like gold.

Her name was Sabrinetta, and her grandmother was Sabra, who married St. George after he had killed the dragon, and by real rights all the country belonged to her: the woods that stretched away to the mountains, the downs that sloped down to the sea, the pretty fields of corn and maize and rye, the olive orchards and the vineyards, and the little town itself–with its towers and its turrets, its steep roofs and strange windows–that nestled in the hollow between the sea, where the whirlpool was, and the mountains, white with snow and rosy with sunrise.

But when her father and mother had died, leaving her cousin to take care of the kingdom till she grew up, he, being a very evil Prince, took everything away from her, and all the people followed him, and now nothing was left her of all her possessions except the great dragon proof tower that her grandfather, St. George, had built, and of all who should have been her servants only the good nurse.

This was why Sabrinetta was the first person in all the land to get a glimpse of the wonder.

Early, early, early, while all the townspeople were fast asleep, she ran up the turret-steps and looked out over the field, and at the other side of the field there was a green, ferny ditch and a rose-thorny hedge, and then came the wood. And as Sabrinetta stood on her tower she saw a shaking and a twisting of the rose-thorny hedge, and then something very bright and shining wriggled out through it into the ferny ditch and back again. It only came out for a minute, but she saw it quite plainly, and she said to herself: "Dear me, what a curious, shiny, bright-looking creature! If it were bigger, and if I didn't know that there have been no fabulous monsters for quite a long time now, I should almost think it was a dragon."

The thing, whatever it was, did look rather like a dragon—but then it was too small; and it looked rather like a lizard—only then it was too big. It was about as long as a hearthrug.

"I wish it had not been in such a hurry to get back into the wood," said Sabrinetta. "Of course, it's quite safe for me, in my dragonproof tower; but if it is a dragon, it's quite big enough to eat people, and today's the first of May, and the children go out to get flowers in the wood."

When Sabrinetta had done the housework (she did not leave so much as a speck of dust anywhere, even in the corneriest corner of the winding stair) she put on her milk white, silky gown with the moon-daisies worked on it, and went up to the top of her tower again.

Across the fields troops of children were going out to gather the may, and the sound of their laughter and singing came up to the top of the tower.

"I do hope it wasn't a dragon," said Sabrinetta.

The children went by twos and by threes and by tens and by twenties, and the red and blue and yellow and white of their frocks were scattered on the green of the field.

"It's like a green silk mantle worked with flowers," said the Princess, smiling.

Then by twos and by threes, by tens and by twenties, the children vanished into the wood, till the mantle of the field was left plain green once more.

"All the embroidery is unpicked," said the Princess, sighing.

The sun shone, and the sky was blue, and the fields were quite green, and all the flowers were very bright indeed, because it was May Day.

Then quite suddenly a cloud passed over the sun, and the silence was broken by shrieks from far off; and, like a many-colored torrent, all the children burst from the wood and rushed, a red and blue and yellow and white wave, across the field, screaming as they ran. Their voices came up to the Princess on her tower, and she heard the words threaded on their screams like beads on sharp needles: "The dragon, the dragon, the dragon! Open the gates! The dragon is coming! The fiery dragon!"

And they swept across the field and into the gate of the town, and the Princess heard the gate bang, and the children were out of sight—but on the other side of the field the rose-thorns crackled and smashed in the hedge, and something very large and glaring and horrible trampled the ferns in the ditch for one moment before it hid itself again in the covert of the wood.

The Princess went down and told her nurse, and the nurse at once locked the great door of the tower and put the key in her pocket.

"Let them take care of themselves," she said, when the Princess begged to be allowed to go out and help to take care of the children. "My business is to take care of you, my precious, and I'm going to do it. Old as I am, I can turn a key still."

So Sabrinetta went up again to the top of her tower, and cried whenever she thought of the children and the fiery dragon. For she knew, of course, that the gates of the town were not dragonproof, and that the dragon could just walk in whenever he liked.

The children ran straight to the palace, where the Prince was cracking his hunting whip down at the kennels, and told him what had happened.

"Good sport," said the Prince, and he ordered out his pack of hippopotamuses at once. It was his custom to hunt big game with hippopotamuses, and people would not have minded that so much–but he would swagger about in the streets of the town with his pack yelping and gamboling at his heels, and when he did that, the green-grocer, who had his stall in the marketplace, always regretted it; and the crockery merchant, who spread his wares on the pavement, was ruined for life every time the Prince chose to show off his pack.

The Prince rode out of the town with his hippopotamuses trotting and frisking behind him, and people got inside their houses as quickly as they could when they heard the voices of his pack and the blowing of his horn. The pack squeezed through the town gates and off across country to hunt the dragon.

Few of you who had not seen a pack of hippopotamuses in full cry will be able to imagine at all what the hunt was like. To begin with, hippopotamuses do not bay like hounds: They grunt like pigs, and their grunt is very big and fierce. Then, of course, no one expects hippopotamuses to jump. They just crash through the hedges and lumber through the standing corn, doing serious injury to the crops, and annoying the farmers very much. All the hippopotamuses had collars with their name and address on, but when the farmers called at the palace to complain of the injury to their standing crops, the Prince always said it served them right for leaving their crops standing about in people's way, and he never paid anything at all.

So now, when he and his pack went out, several people in the town whispered, "I wish the dragon would eat him"–which was very wrong of them, no doubt, but then he was such a very nasty Prince.

They hunted by field, and they hunted by wold; they drew the woods blank, and the scent didn't lie on the downs at all. The dragon was shy, and would not show himself.

But just as the Prince was beginning to think there was no dragon at all, but only a cock and bull, his favourite old hippopotamus gave tongue. The Prince blew his horn and shouted: "Tally ho! Hark forward! Tantivy!" and the whole pack charged downhill toward the hollow by the wood. For there, plain to be seen, was the dragon, as big as a barge, glowing like a furnace, and spitting fire and showing his shining teeth.

"The hunt is up!" cried the Prince. And indeed it was. For the dragon–instead of behaving as a quarry should, and running away—ran straight at the pack, and the Prince, on his elephant, had the mortification of seeing his prize pack swallowed up one by one in the twinkling of an eye, by the dragon they had come out to hunt. The dragon swallowed all the hippopotamuses just as a dog swallows bits of meat. It was a shocking sight. Of the whole of the pack that had come out sporting so merrily to the music of the horn, now not even a puppy-hippopotamus was left, and the dragon was looking anxiously around to see if he had forgotten anything.

The Prince slipped off his elephant on the other side and ran into the thickest part of the wood. He hoped the dragon could not break through the bushes there, since they were very strong and close. He went crawling on hands and knees in a most un-Prince-like way, and at last, finding a hollow tree, he crept into it. The wood was very still—no crashing of branches and no smell of burning came to alarm the Prince.

He drained the silver hunting bottle slung from his shoulder, and stretched his legs in the hollow tree. He never shed a single tear for his poor tame hippopotamuses who had eaten from his hand and followed him faithfully in all the pleasures of the chase for so many years. For he was a false Prince, with a skin like leather and hair like hearth brushes and a heart like a stone. He never shed a tear, but he just went to sleep.

When he awoke it was dark. He crept out of the tree and rubbed his eyes. The wood was black about him, but there was a red glow in a dell close by. It was a fire of sticks, and beside it sat a ragged youth with long, yellow hair; all around lay sleeping forms which breathed heavily.

"Who are you?" said the Prince.

"I'm Elfin, the pig keeper," said the ragged youth. "And who are you?"

"I'm Tiresome, the Prince," said the other.

"And what are you doing out of your palace at this time of night?" asked the pig keeper, severely.

"I've been hunting," said the Prince.

The pig keeper laughed. "Oh, it was you I saw, then? A good hunt, wasn't it? My pigs and I were looking on."

All the sleeping forms grunted and snored, and the Prince saw that they were pigs: He knew it by their manners.

"If you had known as much as I do," Elfin went on, "you might have saved your pack."

"What do you mean?" said Tiresome.

"Why, the dragon," said Elfin. "You went out at the wrong time of day. The dragon should be hunted at night."

"No, thank you," said the Prince, with a shudder. "A daylight hunt is quite good enough for me, you silly pig keeper."

"Oh, well," said Elfin, "do as you like about it—the dragon will come and hunt you tomorrow, as likely as not. I don't care if he does, you silly Prince."

"You're very rude," said Tiresome.

"Oh, no, only truthful," said Elfin.

"Well, tell me the truth, then. What is it that, if I had known as much as you do about, I shouldn't have lost my hippopotamuses?"

"You don't speak very good English," said Elfin. "But come, what will you give me if I tell you?"

"If you tell me what?" said the tiresome Prince.

"What you want to know."

"I don't want to know anything," said Prince Tiresome.

"Then you're more of a silly even than I thought," said Elfin. "Don't you want to know how to settle the dragon before he settles you?"

"It might be as well," the Prince admitted.

"Well, I haven't much patience at any time," said Elfin, "and now I can assure you that there's very little left. What will you give me if I tell you?"

"Half my kingdom," said the Prince, "and my cousin's hand in marriage."

"Done," said the pig keeper. "Here goes! The dragon grows small at night! He sleeps under the root of this tree. I use him to light my fire with."

And, sure enough, there under the tree was the dragon on a nest of scorched moss, and he was about as long as your finger.

"How can I kill him?" asked the Prince.

"I don't know that you can kill him," said Elfin, "but you can take him away if you've brought anything to put him in. That bottle of yours would do."

So between them they managed, with bits of stick and by singeing their fingers a little, to poke and shove the dragon till they made it creep into the silver hunting bottle, and then the Prince screwed on the top tight.

"Now we've got him," said Elfin. "Let's take him home and put Solomon's seal on the mouth of the bottle, and then he'll be safe enough. Come along—we'll divide up the kingdom tomorrow, and then I shall have some money to buy fine clothes to go courting in."

But when the wicked Prince made promises he did not make them to keep.

"Go on with you! What do you mean?" he said. "I found the dragon and I've imprisoned him. I never said a word about courtings or kingdoms. If you say I did, I shall cut your head off at once." And he drew his sword.

"All right," said Elfin, shrugging his shoulders. "I'm better off than you are, anyhow."

"What do you mean?" spluttered the Prince.

"Why, you've only got a kingdom (and a dragon), but I've got clean hands (and five and seventy fine black pigs)."

So Elfin sat down again by his fire, and the Prince went home and told his Parliament how clever and brave he had been, and though he woke them up on purpose to tell them, they were not angry, but said: "You are indeed brave and clever." For they knew what happened to people with whom the Prince was not pleased.

Then the Prime Minister solemnly put Solomon's seal on the mouth of the bottle, and the bottle was put in the

Treasury, which was the strongest building in the town, and was made of solid copper, with walls as thick as Waterloo Bridge.

The bottle was set down among the sacks of gold, and the junior secretary to the junior clerk of the last Lord of the Treasury was appointed to sit up all night with it and see if anything happened. The junior secretary had never seen a dragon, and, what was more, he did not believe the Prince had ever seen a dragon either. The Prince had never been a really truthful boy, and it would have been just like him to bring home a bottle with nothing in it and then to pretend that there was a dragon inside. So the junior secretary did not at all mind being left. They gave him the key, and when everyone in the town had gone back to bed he let in some of the junior secretaries from other Government departments, and they had a jolly game of hide-and-seek among the sacks of gold, and played marbles with the diamonds and rubies and pearls in the big ivory chests.

They enjoyed themselves very much, but by-and-by the copper treasury began to get warmer and warmer, and suddenly the junior secretary cried out, "Look at the bottle!"

The bottle sealed with Solomon's seal had swollen to three times its proper size and seemed to be nearly red hot, and the air got warmer and warmer and the bottle bigger and bigger, till all the junior secretaries agreed that the place was too hot to hold them, and out they went, tumbling over each other in their haste, and just as the last got out and locked the door the bottle burst, and out came the dragon, very fiery, and swelling more and more every minute, and he began to eat the sacks of gold and crunch up the pearls and diamonds and rubies as if they were sugar.

By breakfast time he had devoured the whole of the Prince's treasures, and when the Prince came along the street at about eleven, he met the dragon coming out of the broken door of the Treasury, with molten gold still dripping from his jaws. Then the Prince turned and ran for his life, and as he ran toward the dragonproof tower the little white Princess saw him coming, and she ran down and unlocked the door and let him in, and slammed the dragonproof door in the fiery face of the dragon, who sat down and whined outside, because he wanted the Prince very much indeed.

The Princess took Prince Tiresome into the best room, and laid the cloth, and gave him cream and eggs and white grapes and honey and bread, with many other things, yellow and white and good to eat, and she served him just as kindly as she would have done if he had been anyone else instead of the bad Prince who had taken away her kingdom and kept it for himself—because she was a true Princess and had a heart of gold.

When he had eaten and drunk, he begged the Princess to show him how to lock and unlock the door. The nurse was asleep, so there was no one to tell the Princess not to, and she did.

"You turn the key like this," she said, "and the door keeps shut. But turn it nine times around the wrong way, and the door flies open."

And so it did. And the moment it opened, the Prince pushed the white Princess out of her tower, just as he had pushed her out of her kingdom, and shut the door. For he wanted to have the tower all for himself. And there she was, in the street, and on the other side of the way the dragon was sitting whining, but he did not try to eat her, because— though the old nurse did not know it—dragons cannot eat white Princesses with hearts of gold.

The Princess could not walk through the streets of the town in her milky-silky gown with the daisies on it, and with no hat and no gloves, so she turned the other way, and ran out across the meadows, toward the wood. She had never been out of her tower before, and the soft grass under her feet felt like grass of Paradise.

She ran right into the thickest part of the wood, because she did not know what her heart was made of, and she was afraid of the dragon, and there in a dell she came on Elfin and his five and seventy fine pigs. He was playing his flute, and around him the pigs were dancing cheerfully on their hind legs.

"Oh, dear," said the Princess, "do take care of me. I am so frightened."

"I will," said Elfin, putting his arms around her. "Now you are quite safe. What were you frightened of?"

"The dragon," she said.

"So it's gotten out of the silver bottle," said Elfin. "I hope it's eaten the Prince."

"No," said Sabrinetta. "But why?"

He told her of the mean trick that the Prince had played on him.

"And he promised me half his kingdom and the hand of his cousin the Princess," said Elfin.

"Oh, dear, what a shame!" said Sabrinetta, trying to get out of his arms. "How dare he?"

"What's the matter?" he asked, holding her tighter. "It was a shame, or at least I thought so. But now he may keep his kingdom, half and whole, if I may keep what I have."

"What's that?" asked the Princess.

"Why, you–my pretty, my dear," said Elfin, "and as for the Princess, his cousin–forgive me, dearest heart, but when I asked for her I hadn't seen the real Princess, the only Princess, my- Princess."

"Do you mean me?" said Sabrinetta.

"Who else?" he asked.

"Yes, but five minutes ago you hadn't seen me!"

"Five minutes ago I was a pig keeper–now I've held you in my arms I'm a Prince, though I should have to keep pigs to the end of my days."

"But you haven't asked me," said the Princess.

"You asked me to take care of you," said Elfin, "and I will– all my life long."

So that was settled, and they began to talk of really important things, such as the dragon and the Prince, and all the time Elfin did not know that this was the Princess, but he knew that she had a heart of gold, and he told her so, many times.

"The mistake," said Elfin, "was in not having a dragonproof bottle. I see that now."

"Oh, is that all?" said the Princess. "I can easily get you one of those—because everything in my tower is dragonproof. We ought to do something to settle the dragon and save the little children."

So she started off to get the bottle, but she would not let Elfin come with her.

"If what you say is true," she said, "if you are sure that I have a heart of gold, the dragon won't hurt me, and somebody must stay with the pigs."

Elfin was quite sure, so he let her go.

She found the door of her tower open. The dragon had waited patiently for the Prince, and the moment he opened the door and came out—though he was only out for an instant to post a letter to his Prime Minister saying where he was and asking them to send the fire brigade to deal with the fiery dragon–the dragon ate him. Then the dragon went back to the wood, because it was getting near his time to grow small for the night.

So Sabrinetta went in and kissed her nurse and made her a cup of tea and explained what was going to happen, and that she had a heart of gold, so the dragon couldn't eat her; and the nurse saw that of course the Princess was quite safe, and kissed her and let her go.

She took the dragonproof bottle, made of burnished brass, and ran back to the wood, and to the dell, where Elfin was sitting among his sleek black pigs, waiting for her.

"I thought you were never coming back," he said. "You have been away a year, at least."

The Princess sat down beside him among the pigs, and they held each other's hands till it was dark, and then the dragon came crawling over the moss, scorching it as he came, and getting smaller as he crawled, and curled up under the root of the tree.

"Now then," said Elfin, "you hold the bottle." Then he poked and prodded the dragon with bits of stick till it crawled into the dragonproof bottle. But there was no stopper.

"Never mind," said Elfin. "I'll put my finger in for a stopper."

"No, let me," said the Princess. But of course Elfin would not let her. He stuffed his finger into the top of the bottle, and the Princess cried out: "The sea—the sea—run for the cliffs!" And off they went, with the five and seventy pigs trotting steadily after them in a long black procession.

The bottle got hotter and hotter in Elfin's hands, because the dragon inside was puffing fire and smoke with all his might—hotter and hotter and hotter—but Elfin held on till they came to the cliff edge, and there was the dark blue sea, and the whirlpool going around and around.

Elfin lifted the bottle high above his head and hurled it out between the stars and the sea, and it fell in the middle of the whirlpool.

"We've saved the country," said the Princess. "You've saved the little children. Give me your hands."

"I can't," said Elfin. "I shall never be able to take your dear hands again. My hands are burnt off."

And so they were: There were only black cinders where his hands ought to have been. The Princess kissed them, and cried over them, and tore pieces of her silky-milky gown to tie them up with, and the two went back to the tower and told the nurse all about everything. And the pigs sat outside and waited.

"He is the bravest man in the world," said Sabrinetta. "He has saved the country and the little children; but, oh, his hands—his poor, dear, darling hands!"

Here the door of the room opened, and the oldest of the five and seventy pigs came in. It went up to Elfin and rubbed itself against him with little loving grunts.

"See the dear creature," said the nurse, wiping away a tear. "It knows, it knows!"

Sabrinetta stroked the pig, because Elfin had no hands for stroking or for anything else.

"The only cure for a dragon burn," said the old nurse, "is pig's fat, and well that faithful creature knows it–"

"I wouldn't for a kingdom," cried Elfin, stroking the pig as best he could with his elbow.

"Is there no other cure?" asked the Princess.

Here another pig put its black nose in at the door, and then another and another, till the room was full of pigs, a surging mass of rounded blackness, pushing and struggling to get at Elfin, and grunting softly in the language of true affection.

"There is one other," said the nurse. "The dear, affectionate beasts—they all want to die for you."

"What is the other cure?" said Sabrinetta anxiously.

"If a man is burnt by a dragon," said the nurse, "and a certain number of people are willing to die for him, it is enough if each should kiss the burn and wish it well in the depths of his loving heart."

"The number! The number!" cried Sabrinetta.

"Seventy-seven," said the nurse.

"We have only seventy-five pigs," said the Princess, "and with me that's seventy-six!"

"It must be seventy-seven—and I really can't die for him, so nothing can be done," said the nurse, sadly. "He must have cork hands."

"I knew about the seventy-seven loving people," said Elfin. "But I never thought my dear pigs loved me so much as all this, and my dear too—and, of course, that only makes it more impossible. There's one other charm that cures dragon burns, though; but I'd rather be burnt black all over than marry anyone but you, my dear, my pretty."

"Why, who must you marry to cure your dragon burns?" asked Sabrinetta.

"A Princess. That's how St. George cured his burns."

"There now! Think of that!" said the nurse. "And I never heard tell of that cure, old as I am."

But Sabrinetta threw her arms round Elfin's neck, and held him as though she would never let him go.

"Then it's all right, my dear, brave, precious Elfin," she cried, "for I am a Princess, and you shall be my Prince. Come along, Nurse—don't wait to put on your bonnet. We'll go and be married this very moment."

So they went, and the pigs came after, moving in stately blackness, two by two. And, the minute he was married to the Princess, Elfin's hands got quite well. And the people, who were weary of Prince Tiresome and his hippopotamuses, hailed Sabrinetta and her husband as rightful Sovereigns of the land.

Next morning the Prince and Princess went out to see if the dragon had been washed ashore. They could see nothing of him; but when they looked out toward the whirlpool they saw a cloud of steam; and the fishermen reported that the water for miles around was hot enough to shave with!

And as the water is hot there to this day, we may feel pretty sure that the fierceness of that dragon was such that all the waters of all the sea were not enough to cool him. The whirlpool is too strong for him to be able to get out of it, so there he spins around and around forever and ever, doing some useful work at last, and warming the water for poor fisher-folk to shave with.

The Prince and Princess rule the land well and wisely. The nurse lives with them, and does nothing but fine sewing, and only that when she wants to very much. The Prince keeps no hippopotamuses, and is consequently very popular. The five and seventy devoted pigs live in white marble sties with brass knockers and Pig on the doorplate, and are washed twice a day with Turkish sponges and soap scented with violets, and no one objects to their following the Prince when he walks abroad, for they behave beautifully, and always keep to the footpath, and obey the notices about not walking on the grass. The Princess feeds them every day with her own hands, and her first edict on coming to the throne was that the word pork should never be uttered on pain of death, and should, besides, be scratched out of all the dictionaries.

The Last Dinosaurs

In a lost land of tropical forests, on top of the only mountain in the region, trapped inside an old volcanic crater system, lived the last ever group of large, ferocious dinosaurs.

For thousands and thousands of years they had survived all the changes on Earth, and now, led by the great Ferocitaurus, they were planning to come out of hiding and to dominate the world once more.

Ferocitaurus was an awesome Tyrannosaurus Rex who had decided they had spent too much time isolated from the rest of the world. So, over a few years, the dinosaurs worked together, demolishing the walls of the great crater. When the work was done, all the dinosaurs carefully sharpened their claws and teeth, in readiness to terrorise the world once again.

On leaving their home of thousands of years, everything was new to them, very different to what they had been used to inside the crater. However, for days, the dinosaurs continued on, resolute.

Finally, from the top of some mountains, they saw a small town. Its houses and townsfolk seemed like tiny dots. Never having seen human beings before, the dinosaurs leapt down the mountainside, ready to destroy anything that stood in their way...

However, as they approached that little town, the houses were getting bigger and bigger... and when the dinosaurs finally arrived, it turned out that the houses were much bigger than the dinosaurs themselves. A boy who was passing by said: "Daddy! Daddy! I've found some tiny dinosaurs! Can I keep them?"

And such is life. The terrifying Ferocitaurus and his friends ended up as pets for the village children. Seeing how millions of years of evolution had turned their species into midget dinosaurs, they learned that nothing lasted forever, and that you must always be ready to adapt

The Flower-Breathing Dragon

Once upon a time in a land far, far away, there lived a tall dragon who was bigger than any dragon in any other far, far away land.

This dragon was so tall that whenever the humans who lived at the bottom of the mountain on which the cave that he lived in stood, he'd step on them as he looked through the flowers of his massive garden.

Lest you think a dragon with a garden must be a nice one, you can forget it. This dragon had such big feet that he could never be considered friendly–he stepped on way too many humans for that. No, the only reason he had a garden at all was because when he roared he blew flowers, not fire. His massive garden therefore, was only as big as it was because the mean dragon roared so often.

But, while the smell of one, or maybe even 100 flowers, can be rather pleasant, the smell of one million flowers can grow overwhelming and one day, the dragon could no longer handle the smell.

"I need humans to take these flowers," he thought to himself. "They put them in their houses and wear them in their hair. If I stop stepping on them, I'm sure they'd take them from me."

But even when he tried, he couldn't help but step on the humans as they picked through his garden. He needed smaller feet. A bird that lived in a tree near the cave in which the dragon lived knew this and also knew how to get smaller feet.

"Dragon," he said one day from high above his giant feet. "I was once huge too, but one bite of one special pink flower helped me grow small enough to perch in trees without felling them. You have such a pink flower near the door to your cave. If you eat it, I promise you will shrink to size that will keep you from stepping on humans."

The dragon thanked the bird and picked the flower with his tiny hands. With nothing to lose, he took the birds advice and chewed up the flower. Slowly at first, but quickly at second, he started to shrink, his feet getting smaller faster than any other part of his body. In eight minutes, he had gone from a giant sized dragon to a human sized one. And he was far less mean because of it.

He stepped to his left and didn't step on a human. He stepped to his right and he didn't step on a human. He even jumped high into the air and landed without stepping on a human. And the humans saw this and took note. Not being afraid of being stepped on by the scaly feet of the dragon allowed them to walk into the flower garden and take as many flowers as they wanted for their jars on their kitchen tables and for their hair.

The Dinosaur Pee Camp

Once upon a time there were four dinosaur friends who loved to do everything together. They made forts, they swam in rivers and they played tag. But one thing they had never done was go camping.

One day Stegs decided to change that so he said to his dinosaur friends: "We need to go camping under the stars. We can have a fire and eat hotdogs."

"I love eating dogs," Terry said, but nobody listened because Terry always talked about eating dogs. The rest of the friends just nodded in agreement.

So the next day they packed their tent and walked to a nearby forest. They set up their tent on a flat spot of grass in a circle of pine trees.

"The branches are so high that we can certainly cook hotdogs safely," Bron said to his friends.

"I love eating dogs," Terry said.

The rest of the friends gathered wood and set up the tent. Then they walked for 10 minutes and found a creek where they played catch and swam on their backs. Bron, Stegs and Tri ate the plants from the bottom of the freshwater creek.

"Can we eat dogs now?" Terry asked. And it was time to get back to the tent because it was getting dark and they were in an unfamiliar place. When they got back they started a fire.

"Terry, do not touch the hotdogs," Bron said. "We will do the cooking." And cook they did. They cooked 20 packages of hotdogs over the fire.

"We each have four packages to eat," Stegs explained.

"Can I have 20?" Terry asked.

"No!" They all answered.

So they each had four packages as they talked about how much fun it was to camp. After an hour of eating, it was Tri's turn to ask a question.

"Where is the bathroom? We did all eat four packages of hotdogs, I can't be the only one who needs to use one."

By the looks on his friends' faces, he was not the only one.

"I don't believe we brought one," Bron admitted. "I don't think it would have fit in the tent even if we'd have brought one."

Then, seemingly out of nowhere, a little girl appeared.

"Hi dinosaurs, my name is Leah and I know where there is a potty you can pee on."

"I'm sorry Leah we need to do the other thing," Terry said.

"This is a potty you can pee and poo on. Follow me, it's up a set of blue steps."

All the dinosaurs except for Stegs who needed to watch the fire, followed Leah. It wasn't long before they found the blue steps that led to what Leah kept calling the Pee Fort. They all took turns and even Stegs got a turn to go. Then they went back to their campfire and said goodbye to Leah, being sure to thank her for the Pee Fort.

"That's the last time we go camping without packing our potty," Tri announced before getting up to go to bed.

"I love eating dogs," Terry said on cue.

"We know. Good night."

Like A Longneck

Crutch the dinosaur had a long neck. Longer than his mother's neck and even his father's neck. Being a brontosaurus, he was used to being called long neck by his friends because often they meant it in a plyful way.

But over the years, as his neck grew longer than most of his brontosaurus friends, he started to worry.

"I don't like that my neck is longer than yours," he told Stretch, hid friend with the next longest neck.

"Meh, what can you do," Stretch told him. And really, what was there to do?

"I could get rid of part of my neck. I bet T-Rex would be happy to help me."

"I don't think that's a good idea Crutch. I saw T-Rex help someone with a long tail once and they ended up with a little ball tail that they couldn't use to play baseball any more. I'm telling you, leave it alone. People will forget how long it is after a while."

Crutch hoped this would be the case. The other dinosaurs he considered his friends wouldn't mind, after all they each had things that made them different. Heft had a big stone like thing on the end of tail, Rock had a big horn sticking out of his head and Grit had wings—almost no other dinosaurs he knew had wings! But still there were others who would point and stare and talk among themselves very loudly about his long neck.

One day Crutch was walking through a deep lagoon so he could reach some tasty tree leaves on the far side. On his way, he encountered the usual taunting from meat eating and plant eating dinosaurs alike.

"You could eat the moon with that long neck," a velociraptor called from one bank, nudging his friends to laugh along with him.

"Sorry Clutch," a Albertasaurus yelled from another spot in the lagoon. "I thought you were a tree with that long neck of yours."

The calls had made him sad and as the water got deeper he dreamed about all the things he'd be able to do if he hadn't such a long neck.

He could duck into caves.

He could swing on the hanging vines above the lagoon.

He could spend an entire winter needing only one scarf.

And most importantly, he could walk through a lagoon without being made fun of by others.

But he was quickly pulled out of his dream when up near his ears he heard the cries of another dinosaur.

"Help!" the voice yelled. "I'm stuck and don;t want to fall down the waterfall.

It was true, of course, that there was a waterfall a piece ahead but the trees by its edge were so high there was nobody but he who could reach them. How had another dinosaur gotten up there? Crutch went to find out.

Minutes later he sure enough came across a baby long neck stuck in the top of the tree.

"How'd you get up there?" Crutch asked, his neck reaching up so high he could talk to the little guy almost to his face.

"I climbded."

"And then got stuck it seems."

"Yes, as I walked up all the branches I stepped on fell into the water now there aren't any left to use to climb back down. And I'm a little scared."

"How are you going to get down?" Crutch asked.

"Well, I was hoping you might let me slide down your neck. Do you think you could let me do that?"

"You mean you'd like to use my long neck?"

"Yes, I think I would. If I had as long a neck as you, I'd go all over our land looking for dinosaurs to save from trees. I wish I could."

"You wish you had a neck like me?"

"Yes. Can I slide down now? I'm a little afraid of heights."

Crutch moved his head as close to the little dinosaur as he could and allowed the little guy to hop on and slide down to the bank on which the tree stood.

"So you think I could find a job saving dinosaurs do you?"

"I wouldn't even look for a job, I'd just start doing it. I'm going to go home to start stretching out my neck so I can help you in a few years."

And the little dinosaur walked away with his neck held as high as he could. So Crutch walked away doing the same.

Danny And The Dinosaur

One day, Danny went to the museum. He wanted to see what was inside. He saw Indians. He saw bears. He saw Eskimos. He saw guns. He saw swords. And he saw... DINOSAURS! Danny loved dinosaurs. He wished he had one. "I'm sorry they're not real. It would be nice to play with a dinosaur." "And I think it would be nice to play with you."

"Can you?" "Yes." "Oh, good! What can we do?" "I can take you for a ride." "Let's go!" "Pardon me!" A policeman stared at them. He had never seen a dinosaur stop for a red light. The dinosaur was so tall... ...Danny had to hold up the ropes for him. "Look out!" "He thinks you're a car. Go away, dog. We're not a car." "I can make a noise like a car. Honk! Honk! Honk! Honk! Honk! Honk! Honk! Honk! Honk! Honk! Honk! " "What big rocks!" "They're not rocks. They're buildings!" "I love to climb." "Watch out!" "Down, boy!" The dinosaur had to be very careful not to knock over houses or stores with his long tail. "Hop on!" "Look!" "All who want to cross the street may walk on my back." "It's very nice of you to help me with my bundles." Danny and the dinosaur went all over town and had lots of fun. "It's good to take an hour or two off...after a hundred million years!" They even looked at the ball game. "Hit the ball." "Hit a home run." "I wish we had a boat." "Who needs a boat? I can swim." "Toot, toot!" "Oh, what lovely green grass! I haven't eaten any of that for a very long time." "Wait. See what it says?" "Please Keep Off." They both had ice cream instead. "Let's go to the zoo and see the animals." Everybody came running to see the dinosaur. Nobody stayed to see the lions. Nobody stayed to see the elephants. Nobody stayed to see the monkeys. And nobody stayed to see the seals, giraffes, or hippos either. "Please go away so the animals will get looked at." "Let's find my friends." "OK." "There they are." "Why, it's Danny riding on a dinosaur! Maybe he'll give us a ride." "May we have a ride?" "I'd be delighted." "Hold on tight. Let's go!" Around and around the block ran the dinosaur, faster and faster and faster. "This is better than a merry-go-round!" "Phew! I'm out of breath!" "Teach him tricks." Danny taught the dinosaur how to shake hands. "Can you roll over on your back?" "That's easy." "He's smart." "Let's play hide-and-seek." "How do you play it?" "We hide, and you try to find us." The dinosaur covered his eyes. All the children ran to hide. The dinosaur looked and looked, but he couldn't find the children. "I give up." "Here we are!" "Now it's your turn to hide." The children covered their eyes. The dinosaur hid behind a house. The children found him. He hid behind a sign. The children found him. He hid behind a big gas tank. The children found him. They found him again, and again, and again. "I guess there's no place for me to hide!" "Let's make believe we can't find him." "Where can he be?"

"Where, oh, where is that dinosaur?" "Where did he go?" "We give up." "Here I am!" "The dinosaur wins!" "We couldn't find him!" "He fooled us! Hurrah for the dinosaur! Hurray!" "Well, goodbye, Danny." "Can't you come and stay with me? We could have fun." "No. I've had a good time—the best I've had in a hundred million years. But now I must get back to the museum. They need me there." "Oh. Well, goodbye." Danny watched until the long tail was out of sight. Then he went home alone. "Oh, well. We don't have room for a pet that size anyway. But we did have a wonderful day."

Robot And The Dinosaur Egg

Oh, hi! I was just on my way to go look for dinosaurs. Hey, do you want to come with me? There's one thing we need to do first. We need to go back in time to find a dinosaur! Press a button to start my time machine. Whoa! We made it back to a long, long time ago. Now we should be able to find some dinosaurs. That sounded like a dinosaur. Let's go look! Should we look in the cave, in the trees, or behind the rocks? Do you see any mama dinosaurs around here? Look! There are three of them! One of those dinosaurs might be this egg's mother. To whom should we give the egg? Let's look on the volcano to see if we can find Mrs. P. There she is—up there! Let's yell and see if she can hear us. "Mrs. P! Mrs. P! We have your egg! We have your egg!" I don't think she can hear us. We'll have to take the egg up to her. But how? Should we climb up with my special sticky shoes, take my jet pack, or ask the big dinosaur to lift us up? What a ride! We made it up the volcano to Mrs. P. Let's give the egg to her. "Mrs P! Does this egg belong to you?" "Yes! My egg! My baby! Oh, thank you for bringing it to me." "Mama!" "Baby!" "So cute! A dinosaur baby!" "Thank you for taking care of my baby. Would you like to help me feed him? He eats plants." Let's get the baby dinosaur plants to eat! Should we give him sweet flowers, great big leaves, or leafy branches?

Edward And The Dragon

Edward was the youngest knight in the kingdom. He was still pretty much a boy, but was so brave and intelligent that, without having to fight anyone at all, he had defeated all his enemies.

One day, while riding through the mountains, he came across a small cave. On entering it he found it was enormous, and that inside was an impressive castle, so big that he thought the mountain couldn't be real, and that it must have been a facade put there to hide the castle.

On nearing the castle, Edward heard the sound of voices. Without hesitating, he climbed over the castle walls, and followed the voices.

"Anybody here?" he asked.

"Help! Help us!" came the response from inside, "we've been locked in here for years, serving the castle dragon."

"Dragon?" thought Edward, just before an enormous flying flame almost burnt him alive. Edward spun silently around, and addressing the terrible dragon face to face, said: "It's all right, Dragon. I forgive you for what you just did. You probably didn't know it was me."

The dragon was very surprised at words like these. He never expected anyone to stand up to him, and certainly not in such a brazen manner.

"Prepare to fight, dwarf! I don't give a fig who you are!" roared the dragon.

"Wait a moment. Well, it's clear that you don't know who I am. I am the guardian of the Great Crystal Sword!" continued Edward, who - before fighting - was capable of making all sorts of things up. "You well know that the sword has killed dozens of ogres and dragons, and that if I unsheathe it, it will fly straight into your neck and kill you." The dragon had never heard of such a sword, but this frightened him. He certainly didn't like the sound of something cutting his throat. Edward carried on talking.

"In any case, I want to give you a chance to fight me. Let's travel to the other side of the world. Over there there's a snow-covered mountain, and at the summit there's a great tower. At the top of the tower there's a golden cage where a wizard made this sword. There the sword loses all its power. I'll be there, but will only wait for you for five days."

On saying that, Edward raised a cloud of dust and disappeared. The dragon thought Edward had performed some kind of magic, but he had only hidden in some bushes. Wanting to fight with that impudent knight, the dragon quickly flew out of the cave, towards the other side of the world, in a journey which lasted more than a month. When Edward was sure the dragon was far away, he came out of his hiding place, entered the castle, and set free all the prisoners inside. Some had been missing for many years, and when they returned home everyone praised Edward's great intelligence.

And what about the dragon? Well, can you believe that on the other side of the world there was really a snowy mountain with a big tower on top, and a gold cage on top of that?

Well yes, the dragon squeezed into the cage and couldn't get out; and there he remains, hoping that someone intelligent will one day come and rescue him...

The Cloud Dragon

In the dark lands of the witches and the trolls, there lived, a long time ago, the most terrible dragon that had ever existed. His magic powers enabled him to take on cloud form, so he could move as fast as the wind. He could make himself as light as a feather, and take any form, from a simple lamb to a fierce ogre. And, being a cloud dragon, he was the only creature capable of firing not only flames from his mouth, but also brilliant lightning bolts.

The cloud dragon would attack towns and villages just for pleasure, for the simple fact of hearing people's cries at his terrible appearances. But he only really found true fun when the humans would send one of their knights and heroes to try to kill him. On those occasions he would entertain himself by making interminable rains fall on their armour, or sending little lightning bolts that would scorch the knights and make all their hair stand up. Then he would transform himself into a dense fog, and, the knight, unable to see anything around himself, wasn't even aware that the cloud he was in was rising and starting to fly. And after playing with the knight in the air for a good while, by which point the knight would be completely dizzy, the dragon would return to his natural form, leaving the poor hero floating in mid-air. Then he wouldn't be able to stop laughing, his flames of laughter licking at the knight as he fell at a great velocity into the mountain snows where, hurt, frozen and singed, the abandoned knight would have to search for the long route home.

Only young Yela, the King's youngest son, who had long been famous for his constant naughtiness, felt some kind of sympathy for the dragon. Something inside told him that there couldn't be anyone who was really as bad as that and, as had happened to him from an early age, the dragon would be able to learn to behave well. So, when he went in search of the dragon, he did so without shield or armour, totally unarmed, ready to find out what it was that made the dragon behave as he did.

As soon as the dragon saw the young Prince coming, he began his repertoire of tricks and teasing. Yela found his tricks were really unique, even amusing, and he dared to enjoy those moments spent with the dragon. When Yela was finally dropped into the snow, he got up, singed and hurt, but smiling, and he shouted:

-"Come on! Again! Yee-haaa!"

The cloud dragon was surprised, but it seemed like he had been waiting for that for centuries, since he didn't hesitate to repeat his tricks and even add some more, for the young Prince's enjoyment. The dragon was having such fun that he began taking special care with his playmate, to the point that, when they stopped to rest a while, they did it together, smiling, like two good friends.

Yela not only carried on letting the dragon play with him. The Prince himself started playing practical jokes, putting on shows, and being naughty, and together they created many new tricks. Finally, Yela got to know the dragon's family, only to learn that, despite being hundreds of years old, the dragon was no more than a child; an enormous kid wanting to be naughty and have fun.

And so, the Prince was able to return to his Kingdom on a great cloud in the shape of a dragon, amid the joy and admiration of all. And with the help of children, comedians, actors and buffoons they managed to bring such joy to the young dragon's life that never again did he feel the need to harm anyone for entertainment. And as payment for all the fun the dragon provided rain, shade and fire to the Kingdom whenever it was needed.

Sam And The Dragon

A long time ago there were a lot of dragons around. But... as time passed, there were fewer and fewer, until there were hardly any left. Some died of old age. Some were killed by knights in shining armor, and those that didn't die began to hide away where no-one could find them. Since they had to hide all of the time, they began to change. They got smaller and smaller, until they were no bigger than a little boy. A little boy like Sam.

Sam lived in a town where the weather changed with the seasons, so every fall his family would pack up all of their belongings and move way down south, where it would be warm in the winter. Sam didn't like moving south in the fall and back in the spring, so one day while his family was packing, he said to his mother, "I don't want to move south for the winter. I want to stay home."

His mother told him, "No, we can't stay, because we would freeze to death." But Sam did not believe her because he had never been there when it was really cold out. Sam tried to convince his mother that it would be okay to stay. He said, "It doesn't really get cold. That's just a myth, like dragons and unicorns."

His mother asked him, "What makes you think unicorns and dragons are a myth?" "The old men in the town square said it," Sam replied. "Well, the men in the town square don't always know what they are talking about. Unicorns and dragons are real, and it gets very cold in the winter," Sam's mother said.

Sam decided he would stay home anyway, so when the town began its journey south he hid, so no-one would notice he wasn't with them. When it did start to get cold Sam was sorry he didn't listen to his mother. He became colder and colder...and was very close to freezing when he heard the front door open.

Thinking that his parents had come back to get him, he rushed into the front room, and almost ran right over the little dragon that had come in. Now, Sam had never seen a dragon before so he didn't realize what it was. Sam demanded, "Who are you and what are you doing in my house?"

The dragon replied, "My name is Freness. I'm a dragon and I always stay here when the humans go south for the winter. Why didn't you go south with the rest of the town?" Sam said, "I didn't believe them about winter, so I stayed behind. Now I wish I had listened. I'm cold and miserable and sorry I stayed." Well, Freness felt sorry for Sam and breathed some warm breath on him, to help him get warm. This made Sam feel better, so he decided to be friends with Freness. The two of them stayed there in the house all winter long and had a very good time together. Sam kept Freness company and Freness kept Sam warm. When spring came Freness told Sam that he had to leave.

He said, "People will be coming back and they just won't understand about being friends with a dragon. After all, they think dragons are just a myth." Well, Sam didn't want Freness to leave, so he said, "We could build you a little house in the basement and that way, no-one will know you are here."

So they took some metal and built a little house. When Sam's parents came home they were surprised to find that he hadn't frozen to death during the winter.

When he explained how he had survived the winter, his parents wanted to meet Freness. So, Sam took them down into the basement to meet him.

Well, the next winter Sam's whole family wanted to stay home so they asked Freness to come up and keep them warm.

But Freness didn't want to leave his nice, little house in the basement. He told them, "If you connect big pipes to my little house, and spread them to each room of your big house, I can keep you all warm."

So, they did what he asked, and that kept them cozy and warm all winter long. The following spring when the rest of the town returned, they demanded to know the secret of how to keep warm all winter, and when Sam's family explained, they each wanted a dragon for their own house.

So Freness sent word to all of the other dragons and invited them to come and live in little houses in the people's basements and keep them warm in the winter, and soon, all the people in the town had a dragon of their own.

Before long, word spread of the little town that stayed home in the winter, and shortly thereafter, the dragons multiplied and were welcomed into nearly everyone's home. Still, the men in the town insisted that dragons were a myth. They called the little dragon houses, "furnaces", so they wouldn't have to admit what they really were. But we know better... don't we?

The Great Dinosaur Adventure

James and Matthew are good friends. James is 12 years old and Matthew is 10 years old.

One morning James and Matthew were walking to school when they came across a run-down house. The house had a yellow caution tape around it saying 'DO NOT ENTER!' The boys decided to explore the run-down house. They wanted to have a cool adventure.

In the house they found a weird looking antique clock. They decided to take the clock to James house to show his parents. James pressed a rusty button while holding the clock. Suddenly there was a flash of rainbow light. They started to fall until they landed with a thump on a rock. But the rock started to move. They jumped off the rock in surprise!

They realised the rock was an Edmontosaurus. They have been transported to the Cretaceous period 65 million years back in time! They realised the clock was not with them. They searched for the clock near were they had landed.

In the far distance they saw something shiny. They realised that it was the clock shining in the sun but was surrounded by a pack of Velociraptors. They started to run to the

Velociraptors but the leader of the pack swallowed the clock before the boys could snatch the clock from the pack. The pack disappeared into the rainforest. James and Matthew started to follow the pack but decided to take a different path to the safe. As they started down the path they came across a footprint bigger than any other dinosaur they have seen. Further along they came across a half-eaten decaying dinosaur. This made them scared and concerned about the path they were on.

They started running and realised the path was blocked by what looked like a tree trunk. The tree trunk started to move. It was not a tree trunk! It was a Mapusaurus, which was 14 metres long.

The boys panicked and ran through the legs of the Mapusaurus. It started to chase them. They ran into the pack of Velociraptors. The Mapusaurus crashed out of the brushes and started to attach the Velociraptors.

There was a fierce battle between the leader Velociraptor and the Mapusaurus. The Mapusaurus swung its tail violently and into the Velociraptors stomach this caused the clock to fly out of the the Velociraptor.

Taking this opportunity James grabbed the clock and pressed the rusty button. They were whirled into a flash of rainbow light and was transported back to the run-down house. James threw the clock into the corner and they ran out of the house.

The Dragon Rock

Once Upon A Time, and imagine if you can, a steep sided valley cluttered with giant, spiky green pine trees and thick, green grass that reaches to the top of your socks so that when you run, you have to bring your knees up high, like running through water. Wildflowers spread their sweet heady perfume along the gentle breezes and bees hum musically to themselves as they cheerily collect flower pollen.

People are very happy here and they work hard, keeping their houses spick and span and their children's faces clean. This particular summer had been very hot and dry, making the lean farm dogs sleepy and still. Farmers whistled lazily to themselves and would stand and stare into the distance, trying to remember what it was that they were supposed to be doing. By two o'clock in the afternoon, the town would be in a haze of slumber, with grandmas nodding off over their knitting and farmers snoozing in the haystacks. It was very, very hot.

No matter how hot the day, however, the children would always play in the gentle, rolling meadows. With wide brimmed hats and skin slippery with sun block, they chittered and chattered like sparrows, as they frolicked in their favourite spot. Now, their favourite spot is very important to this story because in this particular spot is a large, long, scaly rock that looks amazingly similar to a sleeping dragon.

The children knew it was a dragon.

The grown ups knew it was a dragon.

The dogs and cats and birds knew it was a dragon.

But nobody was scared because it never, ever moved.

The boys and girls would clamber all over it, poking sticks at it and hanging wet gumboots on its ears but it didn't mind in the least. The men folk would sometimes chop firewood on its zigzagged tail because it was just the right height and the Ladies Weaving Group often spun sheep fleece on its spikes.

Often on a cool night, when the stars were twinkling brightly in a velvet sky and the children peacefully asleep, the grown ups would settle for the evening with a mug of steaming cocoa in a soft cushioned armchair. Then the stories about How The Dragon Got There began. Nobody knew for sure, there were many different versions depending on which family told the tale, but one thing that everybody agreed on, was this:

In Times of Trouble

The Dragon will Wake

And Free the Village

By making a Lake

This little poem was etched into everybody's minds and sometimes appeared on tea towels and grandma's embroidery.

The days went by slowly, quietly and most importantly, without any rain. There had been no rain in the valley for as long as the children could remember. The wells were starting to bring up muddy brown water and clothes had to be washed in yesterday's dishwater. The lawns had faded to a crisp biscuit colour and the flowers drooped their beautiful heads. Even the trees seemed to hang their branches like weary arms. The valley turned browner and drier and thirstier, every hot, baking day.

The townsfolk grew worried and would murmur to each other when passing with much shaking of heads and tut tuts. They would look upwards searching for rain clouds in the blue, clear sky, but none ever came.

"The tale of the Dragon cannot be true," said old Mrs Greywhistle, the shopkeeper. "It hasn't moved an inch, I swear," replied her customer, tapping an angry foot. It was now too hot for the children to play out in the direct sun and they would gather under the shade of the trees, digging holes in the dust and snapping brittle twigs.

"The Dragon will help us soon," said one child.

"He must do Something," agreed another. "I'm sure he will." They all nodded in agreement.

A week went by with no change, the people struggling along as best they could. Some were getting cross at the Dragon and would cast angry, sideways looks at it when passing. The villagers were becoming skinny eyed and sullen.

Meanwhile, the children had a plan.

Quickly and quietly, they moved invisibly around town, picking and plucking at the fading flowers. With outstretched arms and bouquets up to their chins, they rustled over to where the giant rock lay, as still as ever.

The boys and girls placed bunches of flowers around the Dragon in a big circle. They scattered petals around its head and over its nose, then danced around and around it, skipping and chanting the rhyme that they all knew so well.

In Times of Trouble

The Dragon Will Wake

And Save the Village

By making a Lake.

The searing heat made them dizzy and fuzzy and finally they all fell in a sprawling heap at the bottom of the mound.

They looked up at the rock.

Nothing happened.

A dry wind lazily picked up some flower heads and swirled them around. The air was thick with pollen and perfume. A stony grey nostril twitched.

"I saw something," cried the youngest boy.

They stared intently.

An ear swiveled like a periscope.

The ground began to rumble.

"Look out! Run!Run!"

The children scampered in all directions, shrieking and squealing, arms pumping with excitement.

The rumbling grew and grew.

The Dragon raised its sleepy head. It got onto its front feet and sat like a dog. It stood up and stretched, arching its long scaly back like a sleek tabby cat. It blinked and looked around with big kind, long lashed eyes.

And then its nostrils twitched and quivered again.

The older folk were alerted by the screams and shrieks. The ladies held up their long skirts to run and the men rolled their sleeves up and soon the whole town stood together in a tight huddle at the foot of the hill, staring up at the large beast with mouths held open.

"AHHHHH AAHHHHHHHHH!!"

The noise erupted from the Dragon.

"AHHHHH AAHHHHHHHHHHHHHH!!"

The families gripped each other tighter and shut their eyes.

"AHHHHH CHOOOOOOOOO!!"

The sneeze blasted from the Dragon like a rocket, throwing it back fifty paces, causing a whirlwind of dust and dirt.

"AHHHHH CHOOOOOOOOOOOOOO!!"

The second blast split open the dry earth, sending explosions of soil and tree roots high into the sky like missiles, and something else too ...

The people heard the sound but couldn't recognize it at first for it had been such a long time since their ears had heard such tinkling melody. As their eyes widened in wonder, their smiles turned into grins and then yahoos and hoorahs.

Water, cold, clear spring water, oozed, then trickled, then roared out of the hole, down the hillside and along the valley floor.

The torrent knocked over a farmer's haystack, but he didn't care.

The river carried away the schoolteacher's bike shed but she cared not a jot. It even demolished the Ladies Bowling Club changing rooms but they howled with laughter and slapped their thighs. When the flood sent pools of water out towards the golf course, filling up sixteen of the nineteen holes, the men just hooted and whistled and threw their caps up in the air.

What used to be a dirty, brown dust bowl, now gleamed and glistened in the sunlight, sending playful waves and ripples across the lake and inviting all to share.

"HMMMMM," sighed the Dragon sleepily, and showing his perfect movie star teeth. "Seeing as I'm awake ..."

And he lumbered forward with surprising grace and style and disappeared into the cool dark water with a small wave of a claw and flick of his tail.

They never saw him again.

After the families had restored and rebuilt the village, and set up sailing clubs for the children, and scuba diving for the grandparents, they erected a bandstand and monument in the spot where the Dragon used to lay. Every year to mark the occasion, they would bring garlands of flowers and herbs and arrange them in a big circle. The children would have the day off school, for it was known as 'Water Dragon Day' and wearing the dragon masks that they had been working on all week, would skip and clap and sing.

The Dragon helped Us

As We said He would Do

Hooray for The Dragon

Achoo, Achoo, ACHOOOO! And that is the end of the story.

Earthshaker

BOOM...BOOM...BOOM...

The earth shuddered.

Trees shook, dropping leaves on the tidy nest below.

The nest belonged to an iguanodon. As the eggs rolled around, their mother Brenda steadied them with a claw. 'What on earth?' she wondered.

BOOM...BOOM...

Then, through the trees, appeared the biggest dinosaur she had ever seen. It was like a grey mountain on legs. It had a long, long, neck and a long, long tail.

'Who are you?' asked Brenda.

The long neck snaked towards her. Weak eyes in a little head gazed at her.

'I'm Seismosaurus,' said the enormous dinosaur, in a voice so tiny she could hardly hear it. 'I've come to live here.'

'Sei - Seis - ' tried Brenda. 'It means Earthshaker,' said the dinosaur. 'Call me Sizo if it's easier.' 'Well, Sizo, could you please tiptoe?' 'All right,' whispered the dinosaur. He took two more steps.

BOOM...BOOM...

Pteranodons fell out of the trees. A group of hadrosaurs began trumpeting in alarm. George, the old triceratops, came to see what was going on. 'I can't sleep for the noise,' he grumbled. 'It's Sizo here,' said Brenda. 'He's a little bit, um, heavy-footed.' 'Can't you tiptoe?' demanded George.

'I am tiptoeing,' said Sizo in his tiny voice. 'Hmph!' snorted George. 'What a racket! I hope he's not staying.'

'Oh, please let me stay,' begged Sizo. 'I've been alone for ages. I want to live with other dinosaurs.'

'Give him a chance, George,' said Brenda kindly. 'You can see he's a plant-eater. He's not going to eat us, are you, Sizo?'

Sizo shook his head. 'I'll only eat the highest leaves,' he whispered, 'the ones you can't reach.'

'Hmph! All right,' grunted George. 'But only if you remember to tiptoe!' So Sizo settled into his new home.

He liked the other dinosaurs. But he wasn't really happy.

He worried about making too much noise. Although he walked as quietly as he could, his footsteps made the earth tremble. The other dinosaurs blocked their ears and grumbled.

'Tiptoe!' George would bellow.

Sizo tiptoed, but that wasn't any quieter. In the end, it was easier not to walk at all. He just stood in one place for most of the day, eating whatever he could reach.

And life was peaceful, for a while. Until -

BOOM...BOOM...BOOM...

The ground shuddered. Brenda's baby iguanodons tumbled over and began to cry. The hadrosaurs wailed in protest.

George came storming out of the forest.

'Oy, Sizo!' he roared. 'I told you to tiptoe!'

'But it's not me,' protested Sizo.

'It's true,' said Brenda. 'Sizo isn't moving.'

The dinosaurs stared at Sizo. He stood quite still; yet they could hear thuds and crashes.

'It must be another big dinosaur,' said George uneasily. 'Another Sizo.'

'Oh, no!' said Brenda. 'Come with me, children. You don't want to get trampled on!'

All the dinosaurs hurried away into the forest - all except Sizo.

'Another Seismosaurus!' he thought excitedly. 'Another Earthshaker! I wonder if it will be my friend?'

So he set off joyfully towards the noises to find out.

As he walked, the earth shook harder. The crashes grew louder. He could smell a strange, fierce, burning smell.

'Funny dinosaur, this,' thought Sizo.

He came round a bend, and stopped. Ahead of him a hump rose out of the forest.

'That's a huge dinosaur!' he thought.

The ground beneath him trembled.

'It's an Earthshaker all right,' said Sizo.

Then he saw that smoke was billowing from the hump. Down its side ran a glowing river of red.

'It's bleeding!' he whispered.

The thick red river flowed past a tree. It ripped it up, and threw it down with a crash.

Sizo blinked at the river with his small, weak eyes. It wasn't blood. It smelt of rock, and it was smoking.

'I don't think that's a dinosaur at all!' he said.

The smoking river hissed and sizzled. Two more trees thudded to the ground, and burst into flames.

The river did not stop. It kept on flowing through the forest.

'Oh, no! It's heading for our home!' gasped Sizo. 'I'd better warn the others!'

He plodded back as fast as he could. There was no-one around. Sizo cleared his throat, and shouted.

'Danger!'

It was a tiny shout. He tried again.

'DANGER!'

Still nobody heard him.

'Help!' thought Sizo. 'Whatever can I do?'

Nobody could hear Sizo's voice.

But he knew that everyone could hear his feet. So he began to dance.

He started with big, slow steps. Then he danced higher and higher, faster and faster.

Trees dropped their branches. The ground began to crack.

And Sizo kept dancing.

All the other dinosaurs rushed up to stop him.

'I said TIPTOE!' yelled George.

'Sizo, what do you think you're doing?' cried all the dinosaurs.

'I'm dancing,' whispered Sizo.

'Dancing?' said George. 'That's it! You're banned!'

'But there's danger coming!'

'Danger?' said Brenda. 'Where?'

'There's a river of fire coming towards us. It's flowing out of a hill and burning everything up!'

'What?' cried Brenda. 'That's a volcano! We must get out of the way.'

The dinosaurs didn't wait to hear any more. Together, they thundered through the trees. A cloud of smoke followed them. Behind them, burning branches crackled and crashed to the ground.

'Where are we going?' wailed George.

'We need to get to higher ground,' said Brenda.

But her babies began to squeal. Hot ash was falling like rain.

'It's burning us, Mum!' they cried.

'Quick!' said Sizo. 'Come and shelter under me.'

The baby iguanodons crept beneath Sizo. His huge bulk kept the hot ash off them while they walked.

'You'll stand on them!' protested George.

'No, I won't,' said Sizo. He had had so much practice at tiptoeing that he never once trod on a baby's tail.

The dinosaurs climbed to the top of a hill and left the smoke and ash behind.

At last they stopped. Brenda's babies peered out from under Sizo.

'Is it safe yet?' panted George. 'I can't see.'

'Let me look.' Sizo craned his long neck over the treetops. 'Yes, we're safe here,' he said.

'Thanks to you!' said Brenda, gathering her children round her. 'Sizo, you're a real friend.'

'Am I?'

'The best. From now on, you can thump all you like. We won't complain.'

'Yes, we will!' said George.

The other dinosaurs glared at George. He coughed.

'Er, sorry. Thump away, Sizo. You can even dance if you want.'

'All right!' whispered Sizo happily. 'But I promise that I'll only dance on tiptoe!'

The Greatest Love Of All

I lay down, resting my head tiredly on the edge of my nest. The twigs poked at my frill and I quickly jerked my head away and shifted my position. My eggs felt warm beneath me. It had been twenty-seven days since I had lay them. For the past twenty-seven days, I had been keeping watch all time long. It dawned on me that I could faint anytime soon. My head felt like two hundred conifers piled up together and my eyelids were droopy with sleep. I could not get a good night sleep as it felt like there were stones poking me in the back. I yawned, but tried to resist the temptation of sleeping. My mate was out, finding food for us to eat. I hope he was safe. I sighed. My herd had gone out to find another place to stay in, leaving me and a few others. If we stayed in one place for too long, our predators would find us and we would have to fight them to stay alive. We were hunted by the Velociraptors. A feeling of unfairness passed through me. Why do I have to be born as a small dinosaur, a Protoceratop? Always having to stay on guard or else I would die, that was my life. They were likely to come for us again, like they did yesterday. Only one came yesterday but today, I am not too sure. It was better to be safe than sorry, I guess.

My herd mates romped restlessly around. It might seem like an uneventful day but, things could take a turn for the worst suddenly, without you even knowing sometimes. That's why we have to always be on guard. I shivered at that thought, recalling about how one of my fellow herd mate was killed by the infamous Velociraptor recently. Reality is an enemy. Fear is a beast that feeds on my attention. I took a deep breath, trying to help out with the defence. The air smelt damp. My home was covered by the ferns growing on the ground. The ground was filled with small plants and soft grass that was comfortable to lie on.

The chirps and the swishing of leaves were common sounds I heard every day. That does not mean I had a specific routine every day. It is just that every day is different. I have to face different challenges daily. Once my children are born, it would be tougher. I sniffed the air, it was scented with flowers. Like pinecones and flowers. "Bang!" a slight thudding sound came from a distance. What was that? I narrowed my eyes and looked around me. My breathing quickened as I looked frantically around. There were only a few of us here. If the Velociraptor came again, there would not be enough of us to protect ourselves. I frowned and sniffed the air again. It smelt different, like the mixture of smoke and ash mixed together. "Bang!" the sound was even louder now. My heart stared to beat quickly and I stood up and out of my nest. It was coming from somewhere between the tough and rough pine tree. I stood in front of my next, ready to fight. The leaves parted and I breathed in sharply, my heart racing inside me. 'Thud!' A huge foot poked through. A second one poked through too, a distance away. Puzzled, I raised my head. Velociraptors did not have feet like that. My eyes squinted as I looked up towards the sky. There was a long bending stick, or rather, no. it was a neck. Phew! It was just another Diplodocus. My herd mates quickly stepped aside, making way for the humongous Diplodocus. They ate only plants, like us so they were sort of, our allies.

It was quiet, now that the Diplodocus had passed. How I wished I could be like them, being so big and majestic, walking through the forest without having to worry that they would be preyed upon. I sighed and trotted back to my nest. I blinked, trying to keep myself from dozing off into a deep sleep. My eyelids were half closed and my head felt heavier than ever. It was already sort of almost as big as my body. My eyelids drooped down again.

A sound jolted me out of my daydream. Something sharp sliced through my back and a searing pain paralysed my body for an instant. Warm liquid dripped down my back and I sent out a roar of anguish. I should not have been daydreaming. Now I had to pay for the consequences. I growled and turned around. It was not a Velociraptor! It had a slight longer neck and towered higher above me. An Oviraptor! A second claw was reaching towards me again. I ran forward and bit it with my dozens of teeth. The Oviraptor let out a growl of pain. Good, it was hurt. My herd mates had rushed over and bit it with their powerful jaws too. It growled in pain. This moment, another one rushed towards us. I let go and stood defensively in front of my nest. They were after my eggs, those heartless creatures! I opened my beak, showing them my dozens of gleaming teeth. I charged at it and tried to bite it. However, it ran too fast and was heading towards my precious eggs at a tremendous speed with its long legs. No, why did it want my precious eggs? I ran towards it as fast as I as my four short legs could carry me. It was stretching its claw towards my eggs as I instinctively ran into my nest. I flashed out my teeth and opened my mouth big, getting ready to bite it. Its claw came down and I bit it hard, before it could reach my eggs. It scratched at me with the other claw and my feet collapsed in pain as I stood protectively over my eggs. It felt like hundreds of sharp claws piercing my back. They could hurt me all they want, but just not my eggs! I growled and clamped my teeth into its claw. My herd mates had gathered around it too and were biting into its tough and leathery skin.

There was only one Oviraptor left. The other had already ran away. The Oviraptor swung its claws violently like how the tree branches were when they were being blown by the harsh winds. My eyes squinted as I tried to bear the searing pain that seemed to be building up in me. I would do my best to protect my eggs. I would never give up! The Oviraptor tried to push me off my eggs and I held on to the edge of my nest with all my might to prevent myself from being swept off, using my claws. I winced and closed my eyes as more oozing blows flowed down my back. I might die today, but not before I made sure that the Oviraptor had gone away! The sounds of the forest seemed to drain away and my mind started to go wild with the everlasting pain. I bit into its claws with all my might. Suddenly, my teeth closed in and something heavy dropped to the bottom of my mouth. It felt like a sharp claw scraping the insides my mouth. I opened my mouth and let it tumble out. It was really a claw. It was a claw from the Oviraptor! "Roar!" An anguish roar thundered above me. The Oviraptor was falling towards the ground. Yes, this was it. Go on, fall. I heaved a sigh of relief as I heard the victorious thud echoing in the forest. I had done it, we had done it. My eggs were safe, my future babies were safe! I lay down on my eggs and stared blankly at the canopy of leaves above me. I had done it. A surge of victory and happiness flowed over me. Yes, I had done it finally. I closed my eyes and my pains vanished in an instant.

The Funny Dragon

Now most people think that Dragons have wings and they do, but only the Dragon Clan called 'Splitter'. The other clan is called 'Ditot'. That clan is pure dragon, no wings. The Splitters' weak spot is in the middle of the wings. The Ditot clan's weakness is on their feet and the back of their head.

Adam was a Dragon; he grew up in the city of Revet. It is the main city for the Zeos Empire. Adam was very well taught to breathe fire. But he could only make a wall of fire so hot that if anything hit, it would surely melt. He could not use fire for offence.

He preformed fire tricks and he would climb walls to produce the best tricks from the best angle. Many saw his show. It was hosted in the king's great hall. One time the king appeared in the crowd and that is where every thing went wrong.

Adam was climbing up the wall to perform a trick when he lost grip and fell. Fortunately he didn't hurt himself. Then he tried to perform the trick from the ground but nothing came out. The king left with others. Later a messenger came by and said that his permit to the hall was unusable. Soon after hearing this Adam left his small hut and set for the witch's castle.

This was a bad choice, for Adam had never left the city and didn't know that at dusk wild foxes and bears roamed the woods. He could not make it to the nearby city of Orange before dusk. He was walking along at dusk when he was cornered at a cliff face by a pack of wolves. Out came a flashing blade and the wolves lay dead, Karth appeared, who was known in Revet as a hero.

'What are you doing here?' Karth asked

"Heading to Orange," Adam replied. "And then onto the witch's castle."

"Then we have the same business," Karth said. Karth lead Adam through the woods and to Orange. Adam knew not to ask Karth what his business was. They stayed in the Orchard inn. The next day, they gathered supplies and headed for the witch's castle. A small desert lay between them and their destination. It was called Sopson, and being small, it rarely claimed lives.

It was a long hot trudge through the sand but finally they made it to the castle. When they went inside the wisest person in the Zeos Empire greeted them. She instantly said 'you punish yourself too much when it comes to your show and you are pressured by the King. Don't be afraid, just relax'. 'Karth come with me for your things'. That was what the wise woman said. Adam slowly returned to Revet thinking and making sure not to go though the woods at dusk. When he came to Revet he was asked to perform by a messenger. He said yes. Karth was never heard of again.

The Reluctant Dragon

One evening, long ago, a shepherd ran home, terrified. "I saw something terrible," he cried to his wife and son. "It's as big as four horses. It has long, sharp claws, a long pointy tail, and shiny blue scales all over its body." His son looked up from his book. "That sounds like a dragon," he said. His parents got scared but the boy wasn't scared.

The next day, he set off up the hill to find the dragon. "He might be friendly," thought the boy. The dragon was friendly and he was thrilled to see the boy. The boy smiled and sat down and asked the dragon all kinds of questions.

The dragon told stories of long, long ago. "There were dangerous dragons everywhere. And brave knights fought them to rescue Princesses," he told the little boy. The boy came back every day to hear the stories.

But then, the villagers found out about the dragon. They were terrified. The boy ran straight to the dragon and said, "The villagers want to get rid of you!" "But I would not hurt even a fly," said the dragon. That afternoon, the boy heard even worse news. Saint George, the dragon killer was there to fight the dragon. Immediately, the boy rushed back to the dragon.

"Saint George, the dragon killer wants to fight you," gasped the boy. "And he has the longest spear I've ever seen." "But I don't like fighting. I'll just hide in my cave until he goes away," said the dragon. "You can't! Everyone wants a fight!" cried the boy. The dragon yawned. "I'm sure you'll think of something," he said.

The boy walked slowly back down to his village. A crowd of villagers was telling about the dangerous dragon. "He eats ten sheep for breakfast! He burned down five houses," roared the villagers. "It's not true!" said the boy. "The dragon wouldn't hurt a fly!" "But everyone wants a fight," said George. "What can I do?" "Follow me!" said the boy and he took George to meet the dragon.

"What a perfect place for a fight," said George. "No fighting!" said the dragon, firmly. "Not even a pretend fight?" asked the boy. "Maybe..." said the dragon. The boy turned to George, "Do you promise not to hurt him?" "Well, it has to look real," said George. "Will there be feast afterward?" asked the dragon. "There will, and you can come," promised George.

The next morning, lots of villagers arrived to watch the fight. The boy waited nervously by the dragon's cave. They cheered and waved when Saint George rode into view. Soon, a roar echoed through the hills. Flames filled the air. Everyone gasped as the dragon appeared. His scales sparkled and his breathed-out fire. "Charge!" cried George. He galloped hard; his spear held high. The dragon bounded up and they shot past each other. "Missed," yelled the crowd.

George and the dragon turned around and charged again. This time, there was no way they could miss. Finally, after a lot of fight, the dragon slumped to the ground. George towered over him. "Cut off his head," shouted the crowd. "I think the dragon has learned his lesson," George declared. "Let's invite him to our feast!"

And he led the villagers, the boy and the dragon back down the hill. The boy was happy because his plan worked. The villagers were happy because they'd seen a fight. George was happy because he'd won. But the dragon was happiest of all. He had lots of new friends and a full tummy. "Jolly night it's been," he murmured and began to snore. "How will I get him home?" said the boy. "I'll help," said George.

He gave the dragon a prod and they set off up the hill arm-in-arm – the saint, the dragon, and the boy.

Dicky The Dinosaur

Was there ever a creature so sad and befuddled, As Dicky the dinosaur, who'd never been cuddled? With rounded teeth and gentle claws, a lack of aggression was among his flaws. He'd run like the wind at the hoot of an owl, the other dinosaurs would all laugh and howl.

Dicky was ashamed and embarrassed, so swore, to become a much more impressive carnivore. But try as he might, Dicky couldn't change, no bit of success he could hope to arrange. He still had no courage and lacked in spite, and worried himself to sleep most every night. Now lady dinosaurs, they were a fearsome bunch, and poor Dicky never dared to ask one to lunch. He was shy and bashful and would quiver with fear, if a terrifying she-rex ever came near.

But one fine day, from his position of cover, Dicky spied a potential reptilian lover. She saw Dicky hiding behind an old tree, "What a lovely young dinosaur boy," thought she.

"What are you hiding from?" the young lady inquired, "A brachiosaurus!" Dicky said, sounding tired. "But they only eat grass," the girl did presume, "I think this one's confused by my rose flower perfume!"

"You do smell quite lovely," the she-rex did say, "Come take my claw, I'll help you get away." She led Dicky to safety and said, "my name's Bella, would you like to go for lunch, you seem a nice fella."

Dicky and Bella went for lunch, and for tea the next day, they soon fell in love in the most romantic way.

Dicky picked her flowers, and Bella would gush, "My dear sweet boyfriend, you're making me blush!" But Dicky still suffered from a nervous disposition, and the plans made in his head rarely came to fruition.

But he resolved his mind to offer a wedding band, and set out one Tuesday to ask Bella's Dad for her hand. Now Bella's father was a scary old dinosaur, covered in scars from the last Dino war. But when he heard of the love Dicky had for his daughter, it caused even his hardened old eyes to water.

"Dicky my lad, you can have my Bella, with a T-Rex like you, she'll be happy forever." So Dicky trod home and asked her that night, and course she said yes, with the utmost delight. Whilst saying his vows Dicky started to sway, and fainted on the spot in a rather swooning way.

"Such a sweetheart," came Bella's soothing tone, as she picked Dicky up and carried him home. Here we leave Dicky, who'd never had a cuddle, a bed with his wife, as they rub noses; and nuzzle.

9 781801 836401